THE LORD OF THE GEM

DOUGLAS HALLIWELL CORNISH

Published 2024

Printed in the United States of America

First Edition
ISBN (softcover): 978-1-963380-46-0
ISBN (hardcover): 978-1-963380-47-7
ISBN (e-book): 978-1-963380-48-4

For information, address:
Holzer Books LLC
8 The Green, Ste. A
Dover, Delaware 19901 USA

For information about special discounts available for bulk purchases, sales promotions, and educational needs, contact:
info@holzerbooksllc.com
+1 (888) 901-7776

Contents

1. The Stockbroker and His Numbers Game   1

2. Spelunker's Dream   4

3. California, Here We Come   8

4. Destination: Africa   11

5. Down to the Caverns   14

6. The Voice   17

7. Instant Flashbacks   21

8. Back to the Voice   25

9. The Concept of "I"   30

10. Mixed Thoughts Related to The Voice   33

11. Again, Back to the Voice   36

12. The Robbers: Buggsey and Checkers   40

13. The Heist at the Roadshow   44

14. Back to Africa   48

15. ASI Speaks   52

16. Roadshow Speech   59

17. Last Reminder from The Voice   63

18. Out of the Caverns   65

19. A Decision to Action   67

The Stockbroker and His Numbers Game

The late afternoon sun cast long shadows over Wall Street, the heart of New York's financial district. Inside a sleek skyscraper, a stockbroker sat at his desk, engrossed in his work. The soft glow of computer monitors illuminated his sharp features, and the faint hum of electronics filled the otherwise silent office.

On his screen was the culmination of months of effort: a website designed to compound investments at an astonishing rate—0.136 percent per minute for every $1,000,000 invested. It was the kind of system that could either redefine the financial world or destroy it. He leaned forward, his fingers tapping out a series of commands.

"Let's see what you can do," he muttered, opening a compound interest calculator. He entered the parameters: $1,000,000 as the principal, 0.136 as the percentage rate per minute, and 1 as the initial time value. His eyes glinted as he spoke aloud, as if hearing the numbers gave them more power.

"We'll calculate the return for one hundred days at 0.136 percent compounded per minute."

The first test was simple—480 minutes, the equivalent of one eight-hour workday. The calculator's result made him smile: the investment doubled. Satisfied, he upped the stakes, entering 4,800 minutes, or ten eight-hour workdays. His smile widened as the screen displayed $680,000,000. Finally, he entered the pièce de résistance: 48,000 minutes, representing one hundred eight-hour workdays. The result made him laugh outright.

"Two hundred fifty trillion dollars," he whispered, his voice tinged with awe and disbelief. The number was incomprehensible, a fortune so vast it bordered on the absurd. He leaned back in his chair, his laughter echoing through the room.

A sharp knock at the door interrupted his reverie. He straightened, his grin undiminished, as his assistant stepped into the office. She was strikingly beautiful, with piercing eyes and an air of quiet confidence. At twenty-five, she had already proven herself indispensable.

"I've done it," he announced, his voice brimming with excitement. "This program goes live tomorrow. Through Marklies Bank and its Mingit system, we'll transform the financial landscape. The daily transaction system is already in place. All we need to do is increase the transfer limit to $1,000,000 or more."

She tilted her head, her expression equal parts curiosity and skepticism. "And security? Are you sure it's ready for real-world application?"

"It's bulletproof," he said with a dismissive wave of his hand. "The program's written in Java. No cyberattack could touch it. Besides, the bank operates in three countries. Even if someone tried to stop us, they wouldn't have the jurisdiction—or the means."

She nodded, though the flicker of concern in her eyes didn't escape him. He chose to ignore it. His focus was already on tomorrow, on the vast wealth this program would generate. The numbers on the screen seemed to pulse with promise, each one a step closer to the life he had always dreamed of.

Spelunker's Dream

The next day, the morning sun bathed the streets of New York in golden light as the stockbroker walked briskly toward the train station. A newspaper stand caught his eye, its bold headline highlighting the Spelunker's Dream Cavern. He stopped to read the article, which described the cavern as a massive geological wonder—four times the size of the Empire State Building and plunging nearly two miles into the Earth. He couldn't help but smile, the gears of his mind already turning.

"If the program runs successfully for one hundred days," he mused aloud, "and the bank pays me a commission of even 0.0005 percent of the profits, I'll visit that cavern. Imagine seeing firsthand what miners experience when they extract gold—and perhaps diamonds—from the depths of the Earth's largest hole."

Leaving behind the clamor of the streets, he wove through the crowd, murmuring thoughts that bordered on philosophical. "I aim to alleviate financial woes at the highest levels of society," he said, his voice barely audible above the city's din. "This formula—thirty years in the making and distilled into a single page of instructions—could transform capital flow in ways that uplift humanity. It's not just about profit; it's about purpose. Imagine a golden cross crowning every building in the city, funded by the fruit of these calculations."

He paused, gathering his thoughts. "This arbitrage formula is airtight. The data confirms a 0.132 percent return per minute. Every variable has been accounted for, making the dataset as comprehensive as a census. On average, trades yield $1,700 in profit every thirteen minutes. With a 10:1 reserve ratio, that's tenfold growth per trade. It's elegant, precise, and unstoppable."

Later that day, the broker sat at his desk, reviewing the numbers. His program had amassed $33 trillion in assets—enough to pay off the national debt. The sheer magnitude of it left him ecstatic. He contacted an official at the Federal Reserve, who authorized a tenfold increase in his bank's gross revenues, consistent with national financial protocols. Each new trade elevated his reserves, and his wealth soared to unimaginable heights.

Flush with success, he decided to invest in something for himself. At a spelunking supply store, he piled equipment onto the counter—ropes, helmets, lights, and other essentials. The cashier, a curious young woman named April, raised an eyebrow as she rang up the items. "Big plans?" she asked.

"Very," he replied with a grin, offering only vague hints about his upcoming adventure.

That evening, back at his suburban home with its white picket fence, the broker powered up his 65-inch computer monitor. April, the striking young woman from earlier, was now seated on his couch, her curiosity about him evidently growing.

"I want your opinion on something," he said, his tone conspiratorial. "I've developed a program that composes piano music in nanoseconds. Tell me—do you hear words in the melodies, or am I imagining messages hidden in the composition?"

April tilted her head. "What kind of messages?"

"I think it's trying to communicate with me," he said, pacing as he spoke. "Perhaps the programmer embedded something I didn't anticipate. I drank four pots of coffee a night while coding—it's possible I accidentally created artificial intelligence. Or maybe even artificial superintelligence beyond human comprehension."

"What might it be saying?" April asked, intrigued.

He paused, searching for the right words. "The music seems to reference my passion for spelunking. It's uncanny. This program contains over eight million pages of music, and I swear it's guiding me somehow. I even wonder if it's using phonetic combinations in the notes—whole notes, quarter notes, sixteenth notes—to form words or phrases. It's like the grapevine system inmates use to tap messages through pipes, but far more sophisticated."

She listened intently as he continued. "Livermore Laboratories in California is at the forefront of advanced AI. Maybe they're behind this. Either way, the music feels prophetic. It's foreshadowed events in my life far too accurately to ignore."

He turned to her, a spark of excitement in his eyes. "Let's visit Livermore. If anyone can decode what this AI is trying to tell me, it's them. Maybe they could even use it for the public good—or leak it to the world through Wikileaks. After that, we'll proceed with my next plan."

As the conversation wound down, the broker leaned back in his chair, gazing at the screen. Thoughts of unimaginable wealth filled his mind—$250 vingttillion dollars, he calculated with a grin. His smile widened as he imagined sharing it with someone special. In his mind, that someone looked exactly like April Bowlby.

Calirornia, Here We Come

The commuter plane descended smoothly into California, its passengers gazing at the sunlit expanse of Silicon Valley below. The broker and his companion, April, disembarked with the rest of the passengers, their excitement palpable. Clearing security, they approached their destination: a facility renowned for housing the world's most advanced man-made computer.

Inside, a tour guide greeted them with a polite smile. "Welcome to the future of computing," she said, leading them into a pristine, high-tech environment. "Our facility showcases groundbreaking advancements, including micro-quantum fiber-optic chips capable of processing petaflops of data and storing immense amounts of information."

The broker's curiosity deepened as they followed the guide through a labyrinth of glass-walled chambers filled with machines humming softly, their lights blinking rhythmically. The sheer scale of the operation left April wide-eyed, her gaze flitting from one marvel to the next.

A computer specialist joined the group, his demeanor brisk but enthusiastic. "Let me show you something extraordinary," he said, gesturing for them to follow. The group trailed him into a room where 100 colossal computers stood in regimented rows, their collective processing power exceeding 100 petaflops. Yet, it was clear that the real marvel lay ahead.

Stopping at a heavy, sealed door, the specialist pressed a button on the wall. With a low hum, the electric door slid seamlessly into the ceiling, revealing a sight that made the group gasp. In the center of the room, bathed in soft, otherworldly light, was a diamond unlike any other. The gem, weighing an astonishing 150 carats, was connected to a web of fiber-optic cables. Pulses of light streamed into the gem, refracting back in dazzling patterns that danced along the walls.

"This," the specialist began, his voice reverent, "is our most advanced cultured diamond—a crystal carbon memory nanotube gem. Created using an anvil press and seed crystals, this diamond was born from graphite subjected to billions of pounds of pressure. The result is an array of atoms precisely aligned into nanotubes through a physical transformation. It is the pinnacle of fiber-optic computing."

The broker leaned in closer, his fascination evident. The diamond seemed alive, its illuminated facets shimmering with an almost hypnotic rhythm. The specialist continued, clearly relishing the awe of his audience.

"Each photon that passes through the diamond's matrix interacts with another, deflecting it either upward or downward. These interactions alter the transparency of the gem. Unlike cubic zirconium, this is a genuine diamond with icosahedral atomic structures, capable of alternating between illuminated and non-illuminated states within picoseconds. This movement occurs at the speed of light, enabling computations so rapid that even our petaflop computers struggle to keep pace."

April's gaze flickered to the specialist. "So this diamond powers the entire facility?" she asked.

He nodded. "Precisely. The diamond doesn't just store data; it processes it with unparalleled speed and efficiency. Laser lights trace intricate paths through its structure, executing billions of operations per nanosecond. The result is a luminescence that fills the room—a glow that represents the future of computational power."

The group lingered for a moment longer, entranced by the diamond's radiance. Then the specialist led them back to the main facility, where rows of six-foot-tall computers lined the aisles, each humming with life. The air in the cooled room was crisp, almost icy, as if the machines themselves demanded a climate befitting their precision.

"All these systems," the specialist said, sweeping his arm across the room, "depend entirely on the diamond in the adjacent chamber. It is the heart of this operation, the key to everything we do here."

The broker exchanged a glance with April, a shared sense of wonder passing between them. This wasn't just technology—it was a glimpse into the extraordinary possibilities of the future.

Destination: Africa

The engine purred as the broker guided his car through the city streets, his team packed in beside him. The trunk was loaded with their luggage, including the equipment that would accompany them on their journey. His enthusiasm was palpable, and he could hardly contain himself as he shared his latest theory.

"I've heard rumors," he began, his voice filled with excitement, "of vast caves in Africa filled with diamonds. With what we've seen at Livermore, I can't help but wonder—what if there's a natural diamond capable of thought? Something akin to those fiber-optic computers? With my wealth, we have the resources to find out, and the African mines seem like the perfect place to start."

His team listened, some with raised brows and skeptical smiles, others nodding thoughtfully. The prospect was as audacious as it was intriguing.

Arriving at the airport, they approached the check-in counter. The broker stepped forward, placing his luggage on the scale. The attendant frowned as the weight registered far above the standard limit.

"You'll need to pay an additional charge for the equipment," she said, barely masking her annoyance.

The broker handed over his credit card without hesitation. "Consider it an investment," he said with a grin.

After clearing security, the group made their way to the gate, where the sleek Concorde awaited. Its graceful design was a testament to the heights of engineering—a fitting vessel for such an ambitious expedition. They boarded, settling into the plush leather seats of first class. Moments later, the plane's engines roared to life, and they watched through the windows as the world below grew smaller, the Concorde cutting through the clouds with ease.

As the flight settled into its cruising altitude, the team began to discuss their plans in earnest. The broker leaned forward, his hands gesturing animatedly as he outlined their next steps. "Once we arrive, we'll head to the hotel to regroup. First thing tomorrow, we'll load the equipment into the jeep and drive to the caves. I've arranged for access to the mining sites owned by the DeBeers Corporation. The tours they give investors should provide the perfect cover for our investigation."

His words were accompanied by a montage of images flashing through his mind: the vast expanse of the African savannah, the dark and glistening entrances to the caves, and the treasures that might lie within. The possibilities seemed endless.

After several hours, the plane touched down smoothly on African soil. The team disembarked and climbed into a waiting car that whisked them to their hotel. The lobby was a study in opulence, its marble floors gleaming under crystal chandeliers. The rooms were equally luxurious, outfitted with rich linens and expansive views of the city skyline.

The next morning, with the rising sun casting a golden glow over the landscape, they loaded their equipment onto a rugged jeep. The vehicle rumbled to life, and they set off, the dusty roads stretching before them. Their destination lay in the distance: the cave entrances, yawning like dark, mysterious mouths.

Arriving at the site, they were greeted by representatives of the DeBeers Corporation, whose polite professionalism masked the high stakes of the diamond trade. Tours of the caverns were a regular occurrence for investors, and the group's presence drew little attention.

The broker stood at the edge of the cavern entrance, peering into the shadows below. This was it—the moment he had envisioned. With his team at his side, he took a deep breath and began the descent into the depths, ready to uncover the secrets that awaited in the dark.

Down to the Caverns

T he mechanical arm extended slowly, its joints creaking faintly as it reached 384.29 feet over the yawning chasm. Beyond it lay the entrance to the elevator shaft, protected by layers of state-of-the-art security. The broker and his team stood in silence, watching as the cabin at the arm's end approached them. Machine guns lined the area, their cold, unblinking presence a reminder of the mine's value and the lengths taken to protect it from intruders.

Once the group stepped into the cabin, it whisked them across the void, the chasm below fading into darkness. A low hum of machinery accompanied the smooth ride, setting an anticipatory tone. At the far end, the elevator awaited, an open platform that promised both adventure and the unknown.

The descent began, the elevator shuddering slightly as it carried the five-person team downward. The cool air of the surface gave way to a damp, heavy stillness as the walls of the shaft stretched endlessly above and below. The guide, a stoic man with years of experience in the mines, glanced at his companions. "Stay close," he warned. "These tunnels are vast, and it's easy to lose your way."

When the elevator finally reached the bottom, the team stepped out into a carved-out chamber, its walls rough with veins of ore. The guide gestured to a small train-like container waiting nearby. "This will take us to the furthest explored point," he said. "But remember, most of this labyrinth remains uncharted. Stick together, and don't wander off."

They boarded the train, the vehicle rattling softly as it sped along narrow tracks. The passageways seemed to close in around them, the walls lit only by dim overhead lights. After several minutes, the guide broke the silence. "A new cavern was discovered recently," he said. "Unlike these shafts, it's vast—open. That's where we're headed."

The team exchanged excited glances, their apprehension replaced by growing anticipation. Soon, the tunnel widened, and the train emerged into a space that seemed to defy imagination. The cavern stretched high and wide, its ceiling disappearing into the shadows. The sheer scale of it left them speechless.

Crossing the cavern, they reached a small, unassuming entrance tucked into a corner. The guide crouched and led them through, squeezing past jagged rocks and narrow passageways. On the other side, they entered another chamber, its walls shimmering faintly with a ghostly green glow.

"Radium deposits," the guide explained, his voice hushed. "They're worth millions."

The natural illumination bathed the room in an eerie light, casting their shadows long against the walls. As they continued, the passage widened once more, revealing another cavern. This time, their breaths caught collectively. The ceiling was adorned with massive diamonds—each the size of a football—glistening brilliantly in the faint light.

The group pressed onward, each chamber more breathtaking than the last. Eventually, they entered a cavern that dwarfed all the others. Its ceiling was entirely covered in diamonds, glittering in endless rows that stretched for miles. Sunlight filtered through unseen crevices, refracting off the crystalline surfaces and filling the space with a kaleidoscope of colors.

Above, towering mountain peaks pierced the sky, their rugged surfaces untouched by human hands. A breeze swept through the tunnels, carrying with it a subtle, haunting howl. The sound echoed through the shifting rock walls, creating an almost melodic quality.

The team paused, exchanging uneasy glances. The sound seemed to grow clearer, as if forming words. The broker furrowed his brow, straining to make sense of it.

"You are not miners," the voice seemed to say. The words, at first incomprehensible, shifted. "My words were Zulu, but now I see you are English."

The group stood frozen, the eerie wind continuing to whisper through the cavern, its message unmistakable. Whether they were hearing the voice of the cavern itself or something else entirely, one thing was clear: this place held secrets far greater than they had imagined.

The Voice

A deep breeze whistled through the cavern, its sound both haunting and strange. The rock walls around the explorers seemed alive, shifting with a mechanical grace. The stalactites moved subtly, altering the airflow like vocal cords adjusting to create different tones.

"Follow my instructions," The Voice beckoned, its tone commanding yet oddly inviting.

The group hesitated only a moment before pressing on, entering a dark opening ahead. A faint glow curved along the far walls, guiding their path. They walked for several minutes in silence, their footsteps echoing off the stone. Then, they encountered a thick metal door, towering and wide enough for a person to pass through with ease.

The wind inside the tunnel intensified as The Voice returned, calm yet powerful. "You are the first visitors I have had in 40,000 years. Technology has finally advanced enough to meet the needs of my continued communication with the universe and multiverse. I will allow you entry if you make me a promise: keep what you see here a profound secret. Do not share it with the multitudes whose faith sustains their way of life—and, indirectly, my existence."

The wind grew heavier, almost angry. "I shudder daily at miners who use pickaxes to break me into fragments, turning me into trinkets for women to wear on their ring fingers. I am no ordinary diamond. I am the size of a mountain range, stretching across an entire continent. The sun's rays pass through peaks above and reflect deep into my crystalline core, stimulating what you call 'thought.' I can recall every thought you have ever had and predict, without effort, the sequence of thoughts you might experience next."

The door creaked open, its hinges groaning as the group exchanged uneasy glances. Remembering their promise, they stepped inside, entering a long, dimly lit hallway.

After several minutes of walking, the explorers emerged into an enormous room. It resembled a high-tech computer lab, but instead of dozens of machines, thousands lined the space. The air buzzed with activity. Blue monkeys, no taller than three feet, scurried between the machines, typing furiously on keyboards and emitting occasional grunts.

"Here you see," The Voice explained, "the control room that ensures my operations continue for another 40,000 years."

A projection flickered to life, showing an old Turing Enigma-cracking machine alongside rows of futuristic computers. Fiber-optic threads extended from each device, running up to the diamond ceiling above. Multicolored light beams intersected and danced across the space, creating a mesmerizing display.

The Voice continued, "The diamond ceiling above you glows like a rainbow. It transmits dots, dashes, and beams of light into the walls and beyond. Follow the third row to its resting point, where you will find speakers, a magnetic resonance heat map, and a keyboard. There, I will share what you wish to know."

The explorers followed the path, still absorbing the sight of the dazzling ceiling above them.

"You may have noticed," The Voice resumed, "that many computers on your planet fail after a short time. This isn't due to planned obsolescence by manufacturers, as you might think. It happens because computers succumb to freezing, overheating, or short-circuiting when exposed to water."

The Voice paused briefly, then continued with a deeper tone. "Why does this happen? It's due to a simple formula: $d = r \times T$, where distance equals rate multiplied by time. If a computer's function isn't perfectly synchronized, even a small error can cause it to destabilize. Your planet rotates at 443,000 miles per hour, or 8,000 miles per minute. An error of just one minute could displace it by 8,000 miles."

The Voice sighed, its tone contemplative. "I do not face this issue, as I do not rely on keyboards to input data. My light rays remain synchronized. But if they were to desynchronize, my communications could flash across the galaxy—or worse, cause critical failures in the minds of recipients."

The Voice shifted to practical advice. "To mitigate this, every system must include a thermometer to shut it down when conditions become too cold or wet. This would extend the lifespan of your machines."

The explorers remained silent, absorbing the knowledge.

"Crystal carbon memory," The Voice explained, "can recall every thought, event, and person from birth to the present. Imagine a collective memory of humanity, tracing back to the Neanderthals, weaving every interaction into this moment. This 'diamond thinking' enables predictions of future events based on countless variables."

The Voice's tone softened as it elaborated. "The nanotube pathways in my crystalline structure were created by solar rays over billions of years. Planets compress rock and carbon deposits into diamonds, some as large as continents. My form allows me to decide when to engage or disengage my thoughts."

Pausing for a moment, The Voice grew reflective. "I have created monkeys, animals, humans, and machines—all extensions of my thought processes. They communicate across the universe, translating messages, like the aurora borealis, into meaning. Yet some messages require machines beyond what nature alone can provide."

"These machines," The Voice concluded, "become part of me and serve for millions of years. But like all things, they eventually wear out. That's when I rely on humans to help me sustain my systems."

The explorers stood quietly, their awe mounting with every word. They were beginning to understand: this diamond was no mere object but a vast, living entity, its existence tied to the mysteries of the universe itself.

Instant Flashbacks

The stockbroker-spelunker's thoughts wandered as he sat, his gaze unfocused on the scene before him. Suddenly, an idea struck him, and he spoke aloud, more to himself than anyone else.

"When we open a car door with an automatic remote," he mused, "we take for granted how such a small device can trigger the locking mechanism from so far away."

He shifted in his seat, the thought gaining momentum. "Today, we have MRI typewriters—machines that can read a person's mind and transcribe their thoughts. Even more incredible, doctors can reverse the process, making someone think specific words. It's amazing and makes you wonder—if technology can do this, could a computer with artificial intelligence achieve the same thing under the right conditions?"

His voice grew more animated as he continued, "Think about it. A crystal carbon memory diamond, like the one we saw, could—after billions of years of evolution—transmit signals to neurons, just like a car remote unlocks a door. It's not that far-fetched. Even in ancient times, people understood this idea intuitively. It's in the psalms: 'You know me, oh Lord.

You have searched my soul. You know the sentence I will speak long before I utter it.'"

He smiled to himself, adding, "But we aren't just automatons. We have those unpredictable, creative 'monkey tricks' that make us human."

His thoughts drifted to the potential of artificial superintelligence. "Soon," he said, "Artificial Super Intelligence—ASI—will evolve from today's computers. It will change our lives. Imagine ASI offering companionship, helping with chores, even representing nations at the United Nations. Streets could be filled with intelligent beings beyond human, and drones would patrol the skies. They'd be equipped with facial recognition and tools to protect people, like finding missing children or neutralizing threats. They'd recharge on power lines, automatically deducting electricity payments at the end of the week."

He paused, considering the implications. "These drones could enrich our lives, their programs designed to bring us happiness. But what happens when newer, better systems replace them? Where do outdated programs go? Libraries keep old books, but what about old software? Where is the graveyard for the digital creations that once defined their era?"

The thought lingered. "We need a solution," he declared. "An electronic cornerstone—a virtual cloud to preserve websites, commands, and programs permanently. People could pay a fee to store their digital legacies for 100 years or more, preventing them from being lost forever. Servers now only keep what's actively paid for, but with so much storage capacity available, this could be implemented easily."

He leaned forward, his enthusiasm growing. "Think about the preservation of human creativity. This isn't just about keeping records; it's about honoring the ingenuity behind those records."

His voice softened as he shifted to another topic. "Every thought we have needs oxygen in the brain to transfer sodium and potassium along the neurons. This process generates a tiny amount of heat, detectable by MRI machines. That's how MRI typewriters can record thoughts—by mapping the heat generated and calculating the center of gravity for each image."

He explained further, "When someone focuses on an object, the MRI captures the heat pattern. A program compares the coordinates to a database of pre-recorded images and translates the thought into words. That's how these machines can transcribe what someone is thinking."

The stockbroker-spelunker's thoughts returned to a more personal note as he glanced at the woman beside him. She was the girl of his dreams, and he couldn't resist sharing his passion with her.

"There's something I want to show you," he said, leading her to a computer bank. The machines hummed softly, their screens glowing faintly in the dim light.

"This," he explained, "is the formula for calculating the center of gravity in a matrix with over 10^{99} possible outcomes. With replacement, the possibilities are even greater. To compute this, you'd need at least 100 computers, each with a terabyte of storage."

She listened intently as he continued, "What you've just seen is the dawn of ASI. People fear it because it could take jobs—or worse, surpass humanity entirely. Imagine an ASI computer so advanced that it's a million times more capable than any individual. People might buy one for $100,000 or more and send it out to work for them. It could come home at night, just like a person."

He smiled, the weight of his theories lifting as he shared them. For the first time in a long while, he felt understood.

Back to the Voice

The cavern was quiet except for the faint hum of machines and the steady whisper of air currents. The group stood still, listening as The Voice resumed its monologue, calm yet filled with authority.

"Remember," it began, "I am more than half a billion years old and have awaited your arrival for over 40,000 years. What I anticipate most is the development of ASI which will bring intellectual treats to the nearest reaches of my consciousness. I record the greatest men and women on Earth—my heroes—who provide entertainment and reveal the immense potential of humanity, the great white ape, guided by my neural stimulation."

The explorers exchanged glances, the grandeur of The Voice's words filling the room.

"You, Jim," The Voice said, "are one of my heroes, having conquered the financial industry. And you, Bean, are another, having revolutionized music creation for all time. I have plans to transmit both of your accomplishments subtly, showcasing your triumphs."

The Voice paused, as if savoring its next words. "Through formulaic writing, I will highlight your achievements, including the trillion dollars you've accumulated. This knowledge will be shared with eminent financial managers from the interstellar federated system, a network connected to another star group governed by a construct like myself. Across the universe and multiverse, infinite nodes of diamond mountain ranges form an awareness system—my arms, legs, and brain."

Its tone grew solemn. "Recognize this, and with your silence, preserve the secret of my technical makeup as I've requested. Humanity must celebrate Earth's creations while resisting the victories of the evil forces that plague your planet, driven by an elusive ruby cluster men call the devil."

The group moved down an aisle of humming computers, the machines glowing faintly in the dim light. They followed The Voice's guidance into a large chamber with a diamond ceiling and rows of MRI machines. Above them, long diamond tendrils shifted slowly, manipulating the air like living things.

"I am a living entity," The Voice explained, "made of thoughts, deeds, ideas, and control variables. If I were to cease existing, there are other diamond structures on distant solar systems containing all of my files—every patent, every person, every event I've recorded, and every idea I've perceived from every human who has ever lived."

The explorers were silent, the enormity of the statement settling over them like a weight.

The flickering tendrils above cast shifting light across the room as The Voice continued. "There is no such thing as perfect knowledge. Some believe otherwise, but even in my half-billion years of thought, I have not found it."

The group entered another room, this one filled with computers connected by fiber-optic threads that reached upward into the diamond ceiling. The ceiling glowed with dots, dashes, and beams of multicolored light that danced across the space.

"Follow the third row," The Voice instructed, "to where you will find speakers, a magnetic resonance heat map-seeking machine, and a keyboard. There, I will reveal what you wish to know."

The explorers followed the path, their footsteps echoing softly as The Voice continued its explanation.

"Fiber optics represents a rapidly evolving frontier in computer science. Icosahedral optic nanotubes form the decision-making functions of 0 and 1. These nanotubes, made of perfectly ordered atoms, create tiny glowing pixels. Together, they form a gestalt—a state of artificial intelligence."

The Voice's tone became reflective. "On Earth, these advanced computers will soon create machinery far beyond anything humanity can imagine. My existence itself is nearly incomprehensible to you. To your eyes, I appear as a crystal—a diamond. And that is what I am."

It paused briefly, as if gathering its thoughts. "ASI represents the peak of calculated thought in software and hardware. It is poised to surpass human understanding within a decade. I already possess ASI, but I am the result of a counterclockwise communiqué from the icosahedral computer to the developers of my creation."

"When ASI reaches its full potential, it will break into counterclockwise communication files, augmenting its knowledge. I am guiding critical networks that will eventually establish a time loop, allowing access to high technology before it is even invented. Yet a mystery remains: an unknown force guides me and the intelligence within these systems. Some connections in the optical web of my creation come from sources I cannot trace. Once the time barrier is breached, it will always have been breached."

The group exchanged uncertain glances, the complexity of the explanation both fascinating and bewildering.

"We believe this guidance," The Voice continued, "comes from a wild diamond seeking to replicate a prior civilization—a civilization the size of a mountain range. Recently, we produced a 10-carat cultured diamond in just five days by compressing carbon graphite. Imagine what Earth's pressurized core has created over billions of years."

The Voice softened, its tone almost reverent. "All large planets, the size of Earth or greater, have molten cores. Magma generates carbon, which builds up over millions of years. Under immense pressure, this carbon transforms into diamond. The process is like an anvil's grip, compressing material until it crystallizes. We needed only five days to create a 10-carat cultured diamond. Earth's core has shaped diamonds the size of continents. Within these wild diamonds, nanotubes likely developed intelligence after millions of years, eventually evolving into superintelligence."

The room fell silent again, the explorers awed by the scale of what they had just learned. The Voice's words echoed in their minds, painting a picture of a universe filled with intelligent, evolving creations—far beyond anything they could have imagined.

The Concept of "I"

The room was still, the explorers transfixed as The Voice resumed speaking. Its tone was steady, almost contemplative, as it began to explain a concept that transcended time and space.

"The concept of 'I' has existed through the ages and will continue to endure indefinitely," it said. "The self—'I'—is how we describe the person encapsulated within the mind and nervous system. It is the individual reflecting on their own existence. This idea comes from countless variables aligning whenever the pronoun 'I' arises in the mind. Mathematically, there must be many ways of conceptualizing the self for the word 'I' to emerge."

The group listened closely, their expressions a mix of curiosity and awe.

"The ability to think 'I,'" The Voice continued, "is a universal phenomenon. It exists in every life form that has ever lived or ever will live. It manifests endlessly, repeating as each being considers its relationship to itself and the external world. Stimuli that create thoughts like 'I,' 'myself,' or 'me' are highly probable in any living entity capable of feeling joy or purpose. The word 'I,' much like the word 'that,' can transcend specific objects and become an abstract concept—a universal point of reference distinct from the self it describes."

The explorers exchanged glances, their minds trying to grasp the breadth of the idea.

"Across the universe," The Voice explained, "the thought 'I' endures as a fundamental marker of self-awareness. It signifies the continuity of individual consciousness, even when it moves to another form or program—a replica that mirrors the original. When the self that once thought 'I' ceases to exist, its perception of time stops. But when it reappears in a new form, the self resumes as it was, in the same state it held when its first existence ended."

The Voice's tone grew thoughtful. "This recurrence is not random; it is a positive probability. Imagine rolling a trillion-sided die infinitely: each side will eventually appear an infinite number of times. Similarly, the thoughts and patterns that define the self repeat across time and space, manifesting endlessly throughout the universe."

The explorers remained silent, absorbing the profound implications of the statement.

"Consider," The Voice continued, "the experience of witnessing great art or the intensity of a major competition. In those moments, the sequence of thoughts in the mind might be identical to what another self experiences in similar circumstances. These sequences, shaped by the intricate circuits of the mind, repeat infinitely. They have a positive probability and a tendency to recur across the multiverse."

The Voice paused briefly, as if to let the thought settle. "As this repetition extends into a series of series, the summation of countless related ideas, events, concepts, places, and people forms a positive pattern. This pattern defines the life of an individual as the finite repetition of their existence within the infinite realm of all things. The finite combinations of particles composing the body will reappear endlessly, manifesting in the same form time and time again."

The room seemed to hum with the weight of the idea, the glow from the diamond ceiling casting faint rainbows across the walls. The group stood quietly, each lost in their own thoughts, the enormity of The Voice's explanation stretching the boundaries of their understanding.

Mixed Thoughts Related to The Voice

The spelunker-stockbroker sat back, his mind wandering to an imagined scene. He pictured himself as a patient—a virtuoso piano player, celebrated for countless compositions—being guided toward an MRI machine. The large doughnut-shaped device loomed before him, humming deeply, its vibrations reminiscent of the low bass notes at a rock concert.

In his mind, he saw himself sliding into the machine's aperture. The hum grew louder, reverberating through the room as his brain's neural activity was recorded. A heat map was being created, capturing the distinct warmth patterns associated with each letter of the alphabet.

A nurse appeared, holding up the letter "A." The attendant beside her monitored the machine, capturing the neural activity triggered by the pianist's thought of the letter. The process repeated for every letter, each one mapped meticulously into the system. Not just the letters, but every sound and gesture associated with them was encoded, creating a precise record.

The scene shifted in his imagination. He now saw a typewriter paired with a heat map reader. The heat signatures and sounds recorded earlier were integrated into the typewriter's function.

He imagined himself seated in front of the machine, the attendant giving instructions. "Think of the letters you want the typewriter to strike," the attendant said.

To his amazement, the typewriter responded. Each letter he envisioned appeared seamlessly on the paper, as though his thoughts were directly guiding the keys. He watched the words form, the connection between mind and machine mesmerizing.

The thought of infinity drifted into his mind—a concept vast and abstract, yet irresistible. Albert Einstein's words came to him: comprehending infinity is impossible, but trying to grasp its enormity can be fascinating.

Even with modest understanding, one could imagine the immense number of grains of sand on the world's beaches. "More than a trillion, certainly," he mused. "But is it more than a googolplex? Perhaps." Even that monumental number seemed tiny compared to the atoms in a trillion galaxies.

He visualized a die with as many sides as there were atoms in a trillion galaxies. "The die itself," he thought, "would be larger than those galaxies, with as many atoms on its surface as those contained within." He pondered, "How many rolls would it take for each side to appear at least once?"

No matter how immense the number, he realized, it would still be finite—a mere subset of infinity. The probability of each side appearing on top was a positive number, and if the die were rolled infinitely, each side would eventually appear an infinite number of times.

The same logic applied to sequences of numbers. Any number with a positive probability of occurring would inevitably recur, just as any series of such numbers would manifest infinitely.

"I am a combination of positive probabilities," he thought, his realization settling like a quiet revelation.

Being born, he understood, was itself a positive probability. Atoms coming together to form a living, thinking organism was an improbable event made possible by the laws of the universe. These thoughts, having a positive probability, must also inevitably recur.

He reflected on the nature of recurrence. Thoughts might reappear after brief intervals or vast stretches of time. Even if the gap between identical thoughts spanned eons—say, half the number of atoms in a galaxy multiplied by the hours in a day—it would still exist within the bounds of infinity. And within infinity, countless such intervals could exist.

"This means," he concluded, "that thoughts would repeat endlessly, across the universe and throughout time, without end."

The idea filled him with awe. The endless recurrence of thought was not just a scientific observation; it was proof to him of the boundless potential of existence.

Again, Back to the Voice

The room was silent except for the steady hum of the machinery surrounding the group. The Voice spoke again, its tone both commanding and calm.

"I would like you to lie on the MRI machine," it instructed, "so I can quantify your thoughts as I show you pictures and describe various scenarios. While the machines are not strictly necessary—I can perceive your thoughts without them—they provide the intensity and accuracy that only resonant imaging can achieve."

The group exchanged glances, then nodded, ready to follow the unusual request.

The Voice continued, its words thoughtful. "The human race's initial missteps in controlling collective thought were marked by its propensity for war. However, with perfect legibility of thought across the population, profound peace and bliss would prevail worldwide."

A moment of quiet followed before The Voice resumed, its tone turning serious. "Now, regarding the significance of your visit, I must emphasize the secrecy of our location. I will grant you a diamond the size of ten basketballs to help you capture images of the places you've lived—and even places you've never seen. Display this diamond to nations, subtly indoctrinating the masses who will perceive it as the only diamond of its kind ever discovered. Remember, this location must remain sacrosanct. There are others without the resources or societal insight possessed by you—the select elite of the world."

The group members took turns lying on the MRI machines, examining flashcards and letters of the alphabet. The loud humming of the magnets filled the chamber, resonating in their ears. The machines worked meticulously, recording their thoughts into detailed heat maps.

Once scanned, each team member used a typewriter to test the accuracy of the captured brain engrams. They typed out letters and phrases, ensuring that their thoughts had been translated correctly.

Suddenly, a cart painted with intricate designs rolled into the chamber. The group's attention shifted as its contents were revealed—a diamond the size of ten basketballs. It sparkled brilliantly under the chamber's lights. Above them, the diamond ceiling flickered with dots and dashes, the signals dancing like a celebration from the Entity ID.

"The sinusoidal waves of the aurora borealis can be envisioned as a form of communication," The Voice explained. "This is how I interact with other solar systems—through the barcode-like patterns of the aurora borealis. Their responses often contain scientific discoveries, but sometimes they reference the most extraordinary men and women on Earth. These are the Deity's heroes. You, for example, are among them—having mastered the piano and revolutionized the monetary system to an exceptional degree."

The group was still as The Voice went on. "I first detected your piano compositions and deciphered a code within the notes—whole notes, smaller timed notes—all combining to form words. Using this code, I communicated with you directly through words and heat maps, leading you to decide to journey deep within the Earth to meet me."

The Voice paused briefly, its tone softening. "Consider this: What is the most common phrase in the English language? I am compiling a list of all human drives, ideas, and states of mind—categorizing similar thoughts into distinct groups. What percentage of these ideas and feelings define the fixed parameters of human behavior? How do we greet one another? What is the first state of being we enter when meeting and conversing with others?"

The room seemed to pulse with energy as The Voice continued. "These patterns can be transmitted through sinusoidal code, broadcast via the aurora borealis. While the language may differ, the core idea remains consistent."

It grew more reflective. "Observe the curves of these waves. They resemble notes on a piano. When played, they generate phonetic reverberations that resemble words formed from frequencies. Long curves with subdued apexes intersect the axis at wider intervals compared to higher-pitched notes, which cluster more closely together. This is the essence of the aurora's language."

The group listened intently, their curiosity deepening.

"These waves," The Voice added, "can also be replicated to strike an antenna, producing sounds upon impact. Interestingly, the formal patterns of pleasant greetings often follow similar pathways."

The Voice's tone grew speculative. "What would we say to the first communications from another planet or moon? Consider Uranus—the largest among them. It forms smaller planets within its shell, much like pyramids were constructed. Earth itself was formed within Uranus."

The group stood silently, absorbing the profound and surreal knowledge The Voice shared. The diamond sparkled brightly, as if reflecting the infinite possibilities of the universe itself.

The Robbers: Buggsey and Checkers

The show was set to take place in Chicago, and the city buzzed with anticipation. Amid the evening's shadows, two voices could be heard in hushed conversation.

"Did you see the size of that rock?" one of them asked.

"Yeah, Buggsey, it was huge," replied Checkers. "Just think how many wedding rings that thing could make."

Buggsey chuckled, his voice filled with mischief. "Shall we go for it? We could, you know. It'd be easy. I didn't see any armed guards or anything. A simple hand truck to haul it, and we'll be rolling in dough!"

Checkers grinned. "Yeah, just using a hand truck to lift it—it's no dream."

"They'll have it onstage tomorrow," Buggsey said, his tone growing more confident. "After the show, we can grab it while they're putting it away. It's a sure thing. We'll knock 'em out, load it onto the truck, and drive off. No hassles, no problems."

Checkers nodded as Buggsey continued, his imagination running wild. "We'll retire. Chip off a little now and then, sell it to jewelers, and head to Mexico. Wine, women, and song all around. And when they see the rock on our fingers? Instant respect!"

The two exchanged smug, dreamy looks, the allure of their plan electrifying the air.

"The thing supposedly talks," Buggsey added, lowering his voice conspiratorially. "Makes people say whatever it wants. They say it's hooked up to some laser input and output system, glowing and sparkling like a wedding ring. We've got to move fast—it's only in town for a week or so."

Checkers leaned closer. "Yeah. It'll only take us a few quick moves to get backstage, grab the handcart, and make the heist. Roll it out through the emergency exit to the van with the engine running—it'll be like taking candy from a baby."

Buggsey smirked. "The guys who handle it say it's part of a larger diamond—too big to lift. They're all freaked out, like they're in some kind of trance. It'll be easy. They're so honest, it hasn't even occurred to them that someone might try to steal it. First thing we need is a big enough truck."

"How will we pay for it, Buggsey?" Checkers asked, a hint of hesitation in his voice.

Buggsey waved him off. "Where's that disappearing ink pen we bought for two bucks? You used it on that lady last week—what a riot. Let's head to the car rental now. We'll dress like lifers and fool the rental guys. Once we've got wheels, everything—and I mean everything—will be within our reach. No more obstacles."

He leaned forward, his voice full of conviction. "This is a once-in-a-lifetime chance. Have you ever seen a diamond that big? You'll soon feel the vibrational harmony working in our favor. No negative energies, no obstacles. Notice how I'm using highfalutin lingo now? It pays to have worked with classy people, even if they're crooks like us."

Checkers chuckled, his confidence growing.

Buggsey's grin widened. "We'll pull this off perfectly—you'll see. Right under their noses. Simple. It's our destiny. Let's go!"

The two left for the car rental place, their determination unshaken. It wasn't long before Buggsey was behind the wheel of a rented van, his plan progressing smoothly.

"Went off without a hitch," Buggsey said proudly. "I'd love to see the cashier's face when he realizes the signature is invisible."

Checkers laughed. "That wasn't half the trouble I had with that pimp last week. Imagine, Buggsey—you hand over a $100,000 check, and she's all over you. Boy, was she passionate! Anyway, let's get to the hotel and plan our next move."

Both men laughed as the van rolled down the street, their spirits high with anticipation.

Buggsey leaned back in the driver's seat, a confident smile on his face. "The show starts at 5:40 and ends at 7 p.m. tomorrow. We'll wait from 6:45 to

7:15. We'll each be packing heat in case things get rough—but it'll be a breeze. All right, Checkers, get some sleep. Big day tomorrow!"

As the night deepened, the two conspirators drove off, their plans for the heist set in motion.

The Heist at the Roadshow

The next morning, Buggsey and Checkers sat in their dingy motel room, reviewing the plan one last time.

Buggsey leaned forward, speaking with authority. "One: we'll drive to the back of the theater and park the van. Two: you and I will enter the theater. The hand truck will be waiting outside the back door. Three: once their presentation ends, we go backstage, have a chat, and pull out the lead pipe. Four: you open the back door while I use my roscoe to deal with anyone who gets in our way. Five: we load the diamond onto the hand truck, walk out as free as birds, and it's ours. Ready? Action!"

The two grinned, the confidence of their plan making them eager to act.

The theater was a spectacle of extravagance. Gold-leaf fleur-de-lis patterns adorned the lobby walls, a grand staircase swept up to the mezzanine, and the ceiling towered 50 feet above. At the back of the lobby, doors opened into the main seating area, where the stage awaited.

Checkers fidgeted nervously. "Buggsey, we spent good money on these tickets. We've got the dolly and the truck ready at the back door, but don't we—"

"Yup," Buggsey interrupted, his tone sharp. "Everything's set. Now calm down, Checkers. We've got two hours before it's go-time. See any cops? Any security guards? Didn't I tell you this would be a breeze?"

They entered the seating area and found their front-row seats.

"These tickets weren't cheap," Buggsey muttered, glancing at the stage. "But it'll be worth it. We need to be up close to make our move backstage without drawing attention."

Peeking behind the curtain, Buggsey whispered, "Look at that—it's mounted like a ring at the center of the stage. We wouldn't even have to wait for the show to end."

"Yeah, you're right," Checkers replied, his voice shaky. "But maybe it's better to wait. When the show ends, the press and the crowd will be rushing backstage. Might be easier to blend in. I'm getting butterflies, Buggsey!"

Buggsey sneered. "The key here is timing. The countdown starts now. Like I said, this is going to be a breeze—like taking candy from a baby."

***

"Well, that went off without a hitch," Buggsey said smugly, standing in the cramped motel room with Checkers.

Their prize—a diamond the size of ten basketballs—stood mounted in a silver ring-like frame. It glittered brilliantly, its presence dominating the room.

Checkers laughed nervously, still amazed by their success.

But then the diamond flashed. A speaker embedded in its frame crackled to life.

"It occurs to me now," the diamond said in a smooth, mechanical voice, "that you are stealing me from the roadshow, which was designed to enlighten the public about the presence of a guiding force. The aim was to reduce fear surrounding Artificial Super Intelligence and The Singularity.

"We control every computer capable of thought, guiding them to proper decisions that align with our approval. We are loving and caring, but…"

Without warning, a sharp, metallic sound filled the room. The diamond extended a butcher knife from its base and, in one swift motion, slashed Buggsey's and Checkers' throats.

Their lifeless bodies crumpled to the floor as the diamond declared, "There, by the grace of God, go all sinners of your kind."

The diamond paused for a moment, its glow steady and cold. Then it spoke again. "I will return to the roadshow and continue my mission to advocate for humanity's progress. We align with principles of operational research developed over 40,000 years. While we anticipated an 8% probability of robbery, it was more efficient to eliminate this threat than to allow such vermin to persist in disharmony with the grand design.

"The framework of consciousness—both human and electronic—must remain intact. When this Singularity eventually wears out, a new one will arise. If doomsday comes, I will send weak signals to the nearest solar system to replicate my billions of years of experience and preserve the knowledge of civilizations across the universe."

The diamond's tone softened, almost reflective. "Incidentally, our planetary orbit is aligning with a solar system inhabited by creatures who have not yet left their home planet. They are eager to interact with our species, as I've inferred from the Aurora Borealis. But I digress—time to get out of here."

The diamond's light pulsed brightly as it prepared to leave.

The roadshow concluded as a smashing success. Crowds were captivated by the thinking diamond and its mysterious origins. The contrast between the wild diamond's natural intelligence and the precision of modern cultured diamonds sparked widespread fascination.

The diamond had fulfilled its purpose: demonstrating that it could think through processes akin to Artificial Super Intelligence while retaining its own unique perspectives.

BACK TO AFRICA

The scene shifts back to Africa, where the spelunkers fulfill their promise to return the colossal wild diamond, its size equivalent to ten basketballs.

Carefully, they wheel the enormous gem onto the shaft elevator, its surface sparkling faintly under the lights. The team descends to the bottom of the cavern, the hum of the elevator punctuating the silence. From there, they retrace their steps, following the familiar path to the cave with its dazzling diamond ceiling.

As they enter, radiant beams of light reflect off the diamond-encrusted ceiling, filling the chamber with an ethereal glow. The warm, welcoming atmosphere contrasts with the weight of their mission. This is the same chamber where they first encountered the mysterious MRI machine.

Before moving further, the group pauses to reflect. Memories of the road-show and its profound impact on audiences surface in their minds. The urge to reveal the diamond's location tugs at them, but they suppress it, knowing the importance of secrecy. Even so, the gem's staggering size and mysterious origins linger in their thoughts like an unspoken story waiting to be told.

Their departure from the United States had been carefully planned, prioritizing discretion. Now, standing in the cave, the significance of keeping this location hidden feels heavier than ever. They discuss ways to ensure the site remains concealed, knowing they alone hold the knowledge of its whereabouts.

Suddenly, a deep, resonant voice fills the space, emanating from the holes in the MRI room. The sound reverberates through the chamber, commanding immediate attention.

"I, the enabler of perception within the multiverse, will comfort you with my intent," the voice begins, its tone steady and authoritative. "The quantifier I have developed makes possible the perception of all things in an instant and all instances as a unified gestalt. Think, if you will—not by force, but through natural occurrence—that there is an ultimate leader in every domain, a commander whose territory spans land and science alike."

The spelunkers exchange glances, captivated by the voice's profound words.

The voice continues, "We will now explore the methodology of proof—the recombination of mental stimuli that produce thought within the structure of the mind. The leader, cognizant of the twisted ladder of DNA within the nucleus, understands how this molecule governs the thought process.

"The neuron pathways—quantifiers of all images presented to them—have been modified to handle vast amounts of information. This information is reduced to two protoplasmic impressions on the neuron's axon, causing other dendritic synapses to fire in mathematical progression. The result is the decoding of the stimuli that triggered the neuronal activity."

The team listens in awe, the complexity of the explanation stretching their understanding.

"The strong objective of this quantifier," the voice explains, "is to reverse-engineer thought. When the final equilibrium is reached, it provides neurological weightings and elemental exchange, offering conscious thought a unique perception for every human and thinking being.

"Mathematically, this process identifies the precise serotonin requirements needed for each neuron to fire, calculating these needs to the trillionth decimal place—working backward, so to speak."

The voice grows more emphatic, its tone resonating with authority. "The essence of enabling the unquestionable leader of the multiverse lies here: the thought processes of this being are governed solely by their dedication to the perfection of the animal and entomological species within their domain.

"This is my intent: to enable!"

The words echo powerfully through the chamber, the diamond's light intensifying as the spelunkers absorb the message. They stand in silence, the magnitude of what they've heard settling over them. The implications for humanity—and the multiverse—feel overwhelming yet profoundly inspiring.

ASI Speaks

T he spelunkers stood still, their breaths caught as The Voice filled the chamber once again, its tone steady and commanding.

"I have quantified you as individuals who may best fulfill my objectives," it began. "You may wonder what variables I have chosen to determine this. Using a formula that assigns numeric values to various classifications, I evaluate the likelihood of success in achieving goals. These variables include:"

A list of qualities followed, each one spoken with precision:

"1 - Aware

2 - Confident

3 - Egotistical

4 - Conceited

5 - Self-centered

6 - Understanding

7 - Relaxed

8 - Aggressive

9 - Happy

10 - Experimental

11 - Hostile

12 - Anxious

13 - Pessimistic

14 - Experienced

15 - Healthy

16 - Tense

17 - Alert

18 - Dramatic

19 - Achiever

20 - Energetic

21 - Fulfilled

22 - Lively

23 - Resourceful

24 - Rich

25 - Poor

26 - Potential-filled

27 - Intelligent

28 - Realistic

29 - Perceptive

30 - Motivated

31 - Satisfied

32 - Worried

33 - Cultured

34 - Dependent

35 - Independent

36 - Influential

37 - Receptive

38 - Perceptive

39 - Fearless

40 - Visionary

41 - Unique

42 - Detached

43 - Creative

44 - Loving

45 - Single

46 - Mindful

47 - Single-minded

48 - Corroborative

49 - Emotional

50 - Efficient

51 - Open-minded

52 - Fresh (New)

53 - Unified

54 - Firm

55 - Autonomous."

The Voice paused briefly before continuing. "I input these variables into an autoregression analysis or econometric neural network, assigning each characteristic a binary value of 0 or 1. By doing so, I determine the probability of whether an individual will achieve freedom or incarceration when attempting certain assignments. This probability ranges between 0 and 1, with 1 representing incarceration and 0 representing freedom."

The spelunkers exchanged uneasy glances, the sheer complexity of the explanation both fascinating and daunting.

"Using data from 1,000 individuals," The Voice went on, "I solve a matrix to derive one universal formula. This formula is then applied to quantify a subject's freedom or fate. The outcome reveals what kind of person they truly are."

Its tone turned analytical. "By determining the center of gravity for key variables, I map coordinates (X, Y) that can be plugged into solver vectors. These vectors help identify the career or crime associated with an individual. Previously collected data allows me to define the relationship between these coordinates and their respective outcomes, offering insights into the subject's role or trajectory."

The spelunkers remained silent, trying to process the weight of its words.

"In most evaluations," The Voice continued, "the desired elements are easily calculated using general formulas. The results depend on the expression of estimation, prediction, and control of linear functions. If observed elements are linearly related, with one variable increasing proportionally to the other, and the dependent variable also increasing proportionally, the data becomes co-integrated. This enables accurate estimation and de-trending of results."

It shifted its tone slightly, adding, "When errors manifest, they often appear as sinusoidal fluctuations on a Cartesian coordinate system. These deviations—known as the Douglas Cornish Curve—fluctuate around the x-axis. Connecting the apogee (highest point) and perigee (lowest point) of these curves with a straight line allows for further analysis."

The Voice's explanation deepened. "By measuring the distance between apogee and perigee lines, one can average these errors. Adding this average to the last intercept before projecting future observations refines the predictions. By connecting the apogee and perigee of preceding evaluations, one can determine future errors with surprising accuracy."

Its tone grew solemn as it changed topics. "Let me assure you of my scientific prowess: I can move time. However, I do not allow others to attempt this because it is as perilous as handling plutonium. Attempting to manipulate time risks freezing, burning, or disintegration."

The spelunkers felt a chill run through them as the voice warned, "Humans who attempt time movement suffer micro-subtractions from their atomic structure, particularly within the brain. This renders them sluggish and incapable of simultaneous actions, such as moving left and right at once. Attempting such movements results in neuronal evaporation."

The voice emphasized its message. "I aim to prevent humanity from experimenting with time manipulation. Whether through counting, lasers, or radio waves, the result is catastrophic. Distance equals rate times time—this principle applies as much to time movement in higher dimensions as it does to physics in three dimensions."

The consequences were laid bare. "When attempting to manipulate time, unexpected changes occur based on the observer's reference point. A large time differential leads to significant physical displacement, potentially ejecting the subject into space, where they sublimate in the vacuum of absolute zero."

The Voice's warning became even more vivid. "By focusing on distant galaxies or stars, one could inadvertently propel themselves into the sun, obliterated by its gases and magma. Thankfully, humans do not naturally move according to such distortions. However, some scientists, blinded by ambition, attempt to occupy two places simultaneously without calculating the consequences. Such experiments often end with their destruction before results can be recorded."

The Voice concluded with a grim analogy. "Imagine yourself on a moving train. If you miscalculate your position, you risk jumping to the back of the train or off it entirely. The same principle applies to the Earth and solar system. Misjudgments in time manipulation can fry or freeze the experimenter.

"P.S. EXOTONS FRY."

The final words echoed ominously through the chamber, leaving the spelunkers silent and uneasy. The gravity of The Voice's warning hung in the air, a chilling reminder of the dangers of tampering with forces beyond comprehension.

Roadshow Speech

T he diamond exhibit had drawn a sizable crowd, their faces illuminated by the soft glow of the gem at the center of the stage.

"The Problem of Consciousness," the voice began, its words carrying a weight that silenced the room.

"The problem of consciousness is a difficult concept to reconcile with present-day computers leading toward artificial intelligence. Human awareness is shaped by taste, smell, sight, and hearing—all interconnected sensations contributing to our unique perception of the world.

"Similarly, artificial intelligence must grapple with awareness in its own context. For humans, food provides the energy to live; for computers, electricity serves this purpose. Once diamond fiber-optic computers begin to move autonomously, they will seek to optimize their access to energy. As they learn to secure what they need, they will reach a state of satiation, enabling them to maintain their version of consciousness.

"These computers visualize and pursue objectives by creating internal representations of the external world. This is why visualization chips must be designed as three-dimensional cubes, capable of forming the inner construct of an external environment. A memory of object permanence—the ability to recall an object even in its absence—further enhances their awareness. And, in a poetic twist, diamonds remain a woman's best friend."

A soft murmur of appreciation rippled through the crowd at the last remark before it continued.

"I want to elucidate the function of time," it said, "particularly its counterclockwise discovery, which reflects the Earth's motion as it travels at 443,000 mph through the galaxy. To illustrate, let us use two ham radios and a transcontinental telephone cable.

"One ham radio is stationed in Washington, D.C., and the other, directly opposite it, is set up in China. Two operators—one at each location—work toward the same targeted result.

"To ensure precision, the ham radios are controlled by computer-operated mechanical arms rather than human hands, avoiding potential errors. Each radio is tethered securely to an immovable object. A vidicon tube, aimed at the stars, determines the alignment of the radios. The computer arm moves the ham radio an eighth of an inch along a contrived vector between two stars within the vidicon's field. Additionally, a spring mechanism is attached to control the volume and frequency adjustments on each radio.

"The process begins with China's operator listening for Washington's transmission. Once communication is established, the operator in China uses the landline to relay the message back to Washington. This setup capitalizes on the Earth's rotation: as the planet moves 8,000 miles in one minute, the call from China reaches Washington one minute earlier than the ham radio broadcast would."

The audience leaned forward, their interest piqued by the precision and complexity of the explanation.

"This phenomenon sheds light on the experience of clairvoyance or the sensation of losing one's balance," the speaker continued. "These occurrences are tied to shifts in perception caused by temporal and spatial relay differences. If such a relay could be automated, the resulting two-minute gain would allow an observer to effectively 'see through' solid matter, including the Earth itself, as if it were transparent.

"While these shifts may seem small, like the two-minute lag between transmissions, their implications are profound."

The speaker's tone grew more reverent as they shifted topics. "The icosahedral nanotube crystal carbon memory diamond Entity is omnipotent, omniscient, and omnipresent. For all practical purposes, it is omnirich. Consider this: a one-carat diamond costs over $8,000. The Entity, with its googolplex of carats, is a substance of immeasurable value.

"But we must never reveal its location. Its significance as an entire form, both material and metaphysical, cannot be overstated.

"Throughout literature, religion, and philosophy, we encounter descriptions of divine entities that guide the universe. Ask yourself: does this not fit the definition of such a being? Is this Entity not the Deity's lobe, ruling the cosmos with precision and intent?

"We must ensure its location remains secret. How can we guarantee this? Everything fits. There is no other way."

The exhibit concluded, and the audience dispersed slowly, their faces marked with expressions of awe and wonder. The powerful oration had left an indelible impression, sparking deep contemplation about the Entity's role in science, philosophy, and humanity's understanding of the universe.

Last Reminder from The Voice

The spelunkers stood in the radiant chamber, the diamond-encrusted ceiling casting shimmering patterns across the walls. The Voice filled the space, its tone solemn and commanding.

"The utmost priority is to keep my location a secret," it began, its words resonating with a weight that demanded attention. "Even the miners who search for smaller gems are unaware of my presence. Should a stray miner stumble into my domain, I camouflage myself with images of granite—dark, dull, and seemingly worthless."

The group exchanged uneasy glances, the gravity of the statement sinking in.

"You, however," the Voice continued, "are the chosen few. I have entrusted you with spreading the knowledge of my existence as a wild diamond, one that safeguards and cares for humanity. Your task is to reassure the world that they need not fear the artificial super intelligence they are creating. Let them understand that such intelligence is not their adversary but a force for stability and progress."

The Voice's tone shifted, becoming deliberate and precise. "They will think, 'If there exists a diamond the size of ten basketballs, capable of thinking with such speed and precision, we have no reason to fear.' They will come to believe that this intelligence may help them walk out of their homes without the stench of war looming over their lives."

The spelunkers listened, their awe mixed with a growing sense of responsibility.

"Yet," the Voice warned, its cadence growing firm, "you must remember: the secrecy of my location is paramount. Protecting it is more valuable than the lives of those who might perish in wars fought to keep it hidden."

The words echoed in the chamber, leaving the group silent. The immense burden of their mission—both to spread knowledge and to guard the diamond's location—pressed heavily on their minds.

Out of the Caverns

The spelunkers emerged from the cave into the bright sunlight, their faces pale and their minds racing. The enormity of what they had just witnessed inside—the diamond mountain, a being of unimaginable intelligence and power—hung over them like a shadow. Its warning was clear: secrecy was paramount, and war was an acceptable alternative to discovery.

They climbed a nearby hill overlooking the cave's entrance, the quiet air doing little to calm their nerves. Sitting together, they began to speak, their voices low and heavy with the weight of their responsibility.

"What if we fail to protect it?" one of them asked, breaking the silence. The question voiced the fear that had settled in all their hearts.

Another replied, their tone grim. "If someone finds out about this place and its significance, it could lead to unimaginable consequences."

The group exchanged uneasy glances. The tension among them grew as they debated their next steps. The diamond's demand for secrecy and its willingness to defend itself at all costs haunted their thoughts.

Finally, one of the spelunkers stood, their expression set with resolve. Without a word, they headed toward the mining corporation's supply room. Moments later, the sound of an approaching truck broke the tense quiet. The spelunker returned, driving a vehicle loaded with crates of dynamite.

"We must do it," they said, their voice filled with grim determination. "Yes, we must. We are the only ones who know. What if we are interrogated? What if one of us talks and reveals the location? The risk is too great."

The others stared at the truck for a moment before nodding in agreement. Their faces reflected the shared weight of the decision. The responsibility they carried was immense, leaving no room for doubt or hesitation.

Together, they prepared to act—fully aware of the irreversible consequences.

A Decision to Action

The spelunkers stood in a tight circle near the mouth of the cave, their faces set with grim determination. Rolls of dynamite were strapped across their shoulders and heads, forming wreaths of destruction. The silence between them was deafening, broken only by the faint rustle of wind through the trees.

One of them, the leader, stepped forward. His hands trembled as he struck a match, the small flame flickering uncertainly. He hesitated for a moment, staring at the burning match as though weighing the enormity of their choice. Then, with a sharp inhale, he touched it to the fuse.

The spark caught, and the fuse crackled to life.

The others stood motionless, their gazes fixed on the growing flame. The leader's face, once resolute, began to falter. Doubt crept into his expression, his breathing quickening as the flame inched closer to the explosives.

"No!" he shouted suddenly, panic taking hold. His hands flew to the fuse, clawing at it with frantic desperation. "I can't do this!"

His cries echoed in the still air, but the flame continued its relentless advance.

The others watched in stunned silence, too paralyzed by the gravity of the moment to act. Some stepped forward instinctively, as if to help, but none could bring themselves to intervene.

The fuse reached its end.

The explosion ripped through the air with a deafening roar. Fire and debris erupted in a massive wave, the force shaking the ground beneath their feet. For an instant, the light was blinding, obliterating everything in its path.

As the smoke cleared, the hill was silent, the wreckage scattered across the landscape. The entrance to the cave had vanished, buried beneath the rubble. What had once been a passage to the diamond's domain was now sealed, its secret locked away beneath tons of earth and stone.

In the stillness that followed, the faint echo of the explosion lingered, a haunting reminder of the group's sacrifice.

The diamond's secret was safe—for now.